TULSA CITY-COUNTY LIBRARY

P9-CCF-119

BR4R
4/19

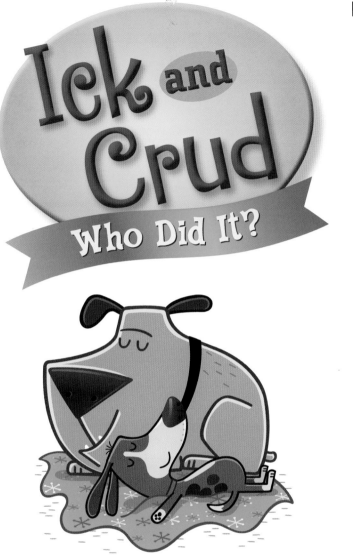

Book 8

Ick and Crud

Who Did It?

by Wiley Blevins • illustrated by Jim Paillot

RED CHAIR ·PRESS·

Funny Bone Books

and Funny Bone Readers are produced and published by
Red Chair Press LLC   PO Box 333   South Egremont, MA 01258-0333
www.redchairpress.com

About the Author

Wiley Blevins has taught elementary school in both the United States and South America. He has also written over 60 books for children and 15 for teachers, as well as created reading programs for schools in the U.S. and Asia with Scholastic, Macmillan/McGraw-Hill, Houghton-Mifflin Harcourt, and other publishers. Wiley currently lives and writes in New York City.

About the Artist

Jim Paillot is a dad, husband and illustrator. He lives in Arizona with his family and two dogs and any other animal that wants to come in out of the hot sun. When not illustrating, Jim likes to hike, watch cartoons and collect robots.

Publisher's Cataloging-In-Publication Data

Names: Blevins, Wiley. | Paillot, Jim, illustrator.
Title: Ick and Crud. Book 8, Who did it? / by Wiley Blevins; illustrated by Jim Paillot.
Other Titles: Who did it? | Funny bone books. First chapters.

Description: South Egremont, MA : Red Chair Press, [2019] | Series: Funny bone books. First chapters | Summary: "There's a new mystery in the neighborhood. Miss Puffy's toy mouse is missing. Will Ick and Crud be blamed, or will the doggie Duo solve the CATastrophic crime?"

Identifiers: ISBN 9781634402644 (library hardcover) | ISBN 9781634402682 (paperback) | ISBN 9781634402729 (ebook)

Subjects: LCSH: Friendship--Juvenile fiction. | Lost articles--Juvenile fiction. | Dogs--Juvenile fiction. | CYAC: Friendship--Fiction. | Lost and found possessions--Fiction. | Dogs--Fiction. | LCGFT: Detective and mystery fiction.

Classification: LCC PZ7.B618652 Icw 2019 | DDC [E]--dc23 | LCCN 2017963474

Copyright © 2019 Red Chair Press LLC
RED CHAIR PRESS, the RED CHAIR and associated logos are registered trademarks of Red Chair Press LLC.

All rights reserved. No part of this book may be reproduced, stored in an information or retrieval system, or transmitted in any form by any means, electronic, mechanical including photocopying, recording, or otherwise without the prior written permission from the Publisher. For permissions, contact info@redchairpress.com

Printed in the United States of America
1018 1P CGBS19

Table of Contents

Meet the Characters

Ick

Crud

Miss Puffy

Bob

Mrs. Martin

The Knock

KNOCK! KNOCK! KNOCK!

"Who is pounding on the door?" asked Ick.

"Come on, Bob," barked Crud. "Open that door."

"Maybe it's someone bringing yummy treats," said Ick. And he licked his lips.

"It's just Mrs. Martin," said Crud.

"What's wrong with her face?" asked Ick.

"It's all scrunchy and red."

"RUN!" barked Crud.

The two dashed under a table. Crud poked out his nose. Ick poked out his tail.

"Where are Ick and Crud?" shouted Mrs. Martin.

"Uh-oh," whispered Crud.

"Someone stole a toy mouse from my sweet Miss Puffy. She was playing with it by the fence. And now it's gone, gone, gone! She's so upset she can barely *meow*."

"Oh, no," said Bob. Then he snapped his fingers. "Come on out, boys, now."

Ick and Crud waddled to Bob's feet.
But neither could look at him.

"Boys, did one of you take something
that doesn't belong to you?"

Crud shook his head. But his tail pointed to Ick. Ick shook his tail. But his paw pointed to Crud.

Bob squatted to look them in the face. "Well, one of you needs to find it. OR ELSE!"

The Search

"What does 'OR ELSE' mean?" whispered Ick.

"It's what Bob says when he can't think of something to say," said Crud. "And it's not good."

Bob turned to Mrs. Martin. "If it's here, we'll find it."

"I should think so," said Mrs. Martin. And she left in a huff.

"Where did you hide Miss Puffy's toy?"
asked Crud.

"I didn't take it," said Ick. "Didn't you
take it?"

"Of course not," said Crud. "She put it
in her mouth. *Ewww!*"

"So, what do we do?" asked Ick.

"We better find it," said Crud.

"How?" asked Ick.

"If it's here, our nose will know," said Crud.

"Yes," said Ick. "Let's leave no stone unturned. Where do we begin looking?"

"How about Bob's room?" said Crud.

"There are no stones in there," said Ick.

"No, but there are lots of hiding places," said Crud. "Are you ready?"

"I will if you will, buddy," said Ick.

The two raced into Bob's room. Crud pulled open drawers. Ick jumped in and kicked out whatever he found inside. Socks with holes. Shirts with rips. Old green and pink underpants.

"No cat toys here," said Ick.

"No," said Crud. "But Bob really needs some new clothes."

"Now what?" asked Ick.

"Let's look on the bed," said Crud.

Crud tossed off the pillows. Then he slipped under the covers. "Nothing here," he barked. But it sounded like a low rumble.

Ick looked up and saw the big bump on the bed. "AAAAAGH! A giant bedbug!" he screamed and darted under the bed.

Crud wiggled to the end. Then rolled off. He landed upside-down on the floor.

"AAAAAGH!" yelled Ick as he looked out at Crud's upside-down face.

"It's only me, buddy," said Crud.

"Hey," said Ick. "Look what I found. Dog treats!"

"So this is where he hides them," said Crud. He tipped over a box and chomped on a big bone.

"It's so cozy down here," said Ick.

"Yes," said Crud. "I think it's time for a nap."

"Okay," said Ick. "We have nothing better to do." The two snuggled under the bed. And soon they were snoring.

"WHAT...HAPPENED...HERE?!"
shouted Bob. Crud and Ick shot up.

"Ow-wee," barked Crud as he bumped
his head. "Eee-ow," yelped Ick.

"Get out here now," said Bob.
"OR ELSE!"

"Uh-oh," whispered Crud.

"He said 'OR ELSE' again," whispered
Ick.

Just then Bob grabbed the two and
slid them from under the bed.

"Outside, outside, outside!" he said.
Bob pointed to the door. "Go!"

The Clue

"**W**hy did Bob send us outside?" asked Ick.

"Maybe he wants us to search in the yard now," said Crud.

Just then a small shadow moved above them.

Crud and Ick slowly looked up.

"Oh, ick," said Crud.

"Oh, crud," said Ick.

Miss Puffy slumped on the fence. She let out a long, slow sigh: *meow-oh-my.*

"Look," said Ick. "She's so sad she can't even lick her paws like they're lollipops."

"Well," said Crud. "I can't look at her droopy face all day. Let's keep going."

Miss Puffy flicked her tail back and forth. Then she let out another long, slow sigh. *Meow-oh-why.*

Crud began sniffing the grass.

"Hey buddy," he barked. "I think I smell something."

"Sorry," said Ick.

"No, this is a good smell," said Crud. "Follow me."

The two went sniff, sniff, sniffing.
Up the yard. Down the yard. And in a
zig-zag.

"Hey," said Ick. "Stop the doggie door."

"What?" asked Crud.

"I think I found something," said Ick.
"What is this?"

Crud looked closer. He took in a deep sniff and sneezed. Then he licked the little piece of gray. "Very interesting," he said. "I think you found our first clue."

"Clue to what?" asked Ick.

"A clue to find the missing toy," said Crud.

"What missing toy?" asked Ick.

"Miss Puffy's toy mouse," said Crud.

"Oh right, we need to find that," said Ick. "Don't we?"

"Yes," said Crud. "And we don't have much time. Hurry!"

Success?

"**W**here are we going so fast?" asked Ick.

"Follow the path of gray fuzz," said Crud.

"Why?" asked Ick.

"Each gray fuzz ball is a piece of Miss Puffy's toy. These pieces will lead us to it. And to the thief!"

"The thief?" asked Ick. He skidded to a stop. "I don't want to meet a thief! What will we do when we find this *thing* you call a thief? I'm too young to meet a thief. I'm too pretty to meet a thief. I'm...I'm...I'm too important to Bob."

"We'll cross that doggie path when we get there," said Crud. "It's time to solve the crime." Crud quickly twisted his head. "Do you see what I see?"

"A tree?" asked Ick.

"No," said Crud.

"That flea on your tail?" asked Ick.

"No," said Crud.

"How big your butt is getting?" asked Ick.

"*Really* no," said Crud. Then he pointed to the corner of the yard.

25

Ruff. Cough," yelped Ick. Bob and Mrs. Martin heard the noise. They raced to the back of the yard. Miss Puffy slinked closer on the fence.

"Oh, me-oh-my," yelled Mrs. Martin. "It's a nest of baby rabbits."

"Yes," said Bob. "The mother rabbit must have dragged Miss Puffy's toy mouse here. Look at how the baby rabbits are snuggled around it."

Miss Puffy let out a hiss and a loud *ACK*! Then she shot off toward the house.

"I guess I'll need to get her a new toy," said Mrs. Martin. She turned to Ick and Crud. "Thank you for finding this. I was sure one of you had taken it."

"I thought it was Ick," barked Crud.
And he pointed his tail to Ick.

"I thought it was Crud," barked Ick.
And he pointed his paw to Crud.

Then the two butt-bumped and headed
back to the house.

"Not so fast, boys," said Bob. He pointed to the far side of the yard.

"Looks like we're in the doghouse again," said Crud.

"That's okay," said Ick. "Bob has a lot of cleaning to do in his room. I don't want to sleep in that big mess."

"Me neither," said Crud.

So, the two waddled to the doghouse.
There they snuggled and took another
long, snore-filled nap. Why? Because that's
what best friends do after solving a crime.